Nadina

Disney's

MICKEY MOUSE STORIES

Including *Mickey Mouse Heads for the Sky, Mickey Mouse and Goofy:
The Big Bear Scare, Mickey Mouse: Those Were the Days*

A GOLDEN BOOK • NEW YORK
Western Publishing Company, Inc., Racine, Wisconsin 53404

Mickey Mouse Heads for the Sky

One day when Mickey Mouse was driving along in his car, a plane whizzed by above him.

"I'd like to zoom across the sky, too," said Mickey. "And I know just how I can do it!"

First Mickey rushed off to the store to do some shopping. "Do you sell clothes for pilots here?" he asked the clerk.

"Yes, we do," she said.

Mickey bought himself a pilot's leather jacket,

a cap,

and a very nifty scarf.

"I look like a pilot already," Mickey said with a grin.

The next day Mickey went to the airport for his first flying lesson. He met his teacher, "Ducky" Lindy.

"I bet it's really easy to fly," said Mickey. "Birds fly just by flapping their wings."

"That's true," said Ducky. "But an airplane is pretty complicated."

Mickey sat next to Ducky in the cockpit. "Oh, my," Mickey said with a sigh. "Look at all those knobs and buttons. How will I ever remember them all?"

"By practicing," answered his teacher. "Let's begin right away.

"Now watch me carefully as we prepare for takeoff," said Ducky. He punched buttons and pulled knobs and pushed a little stick.

The plane rolled faster and faster—until it left the ground!

"Whoopee!" yelled Mickey.

"Now," said Ducky, "you take the controls, and I'll tell you what to do."

Mickey did everything that Ducky said. "I can't believe it," Mickey cried after a little while. "I'm actually flying a plane!"

Mickey had lesson after lesson. He wanted to be the best pilot ever.

One day Minnie said, "Mickey, I haven't seen you at all lately. Won't you come swimming with me?"

"I can't," Mickey told her. "I'm much too busy learning how to fly."

"Oh," said Minnie sadly. She went to the swimming pool without him.

At his lesson that day, Mickey learned what to do if the plane went into a spiral.

Mickey got very dizzy, but he did everything right.

A few days later Goofy asked Mickey to play baseball with him. "You're the best pitcher I know," said Goofy.

"I'd really like to play," said Mickey, "but today I'm going to learn to fly upside down!"

"Upside down!" said Goofy. "Gawrsh!"

Mickey flew upside down perfectly.

"Good for you," said Ducky. "Soon you'll be ready for your first solo flight."

"Gosh!" said Mickey. "I love flying so much, I wish we could stay up forever."

"All planes have to land sooner or later," said Ducky.

Mickey headed back toward the airport. He passed the park where Donald Duck and Goofy were playing tennis. Then he passed Minnie's backyard, where Minnie and Daisy were playing volleyball.

All his friends looked small and far away, but they seemed to be having fun. Mickey wished that he were having fun with them. But he had to concentrate on flying!

"Hey, Mickey!" said Donald a few days later.
"Today we're having the last picnic of the summer.
Don't forget to come."

"I'll try," Mickey told Donald. "But today's the day
of my first solo flight. If I do everything right, I'll be an
official pilot."

Mickey rushed to the airport. He felt very nervous and excited.

"Good luck on your solo flight," said Ducky.

Mickey's takeoff was perfect. Then he flew the plane higher and higher. He did all the special flying he had learned. He tried his best, and he did it all just right.

"You pass the test!" Ducky told him over the radio. "Now, why don't you spend the afternoon up in the sky?"

"Thanks!" said Mickey. "I feel so proud! I wish my friends were here with me."

Mickey flew for a while, but he was getting lonely all by himself in the big sky. Suddenly Mickey had an idea. "Minnie and Goofy and Donald and Daisy and Pluto *can* be with me. All I have to do is find the place where they're having their picnic."

Mickey flew over the tennis courts, but all he saw were nets.

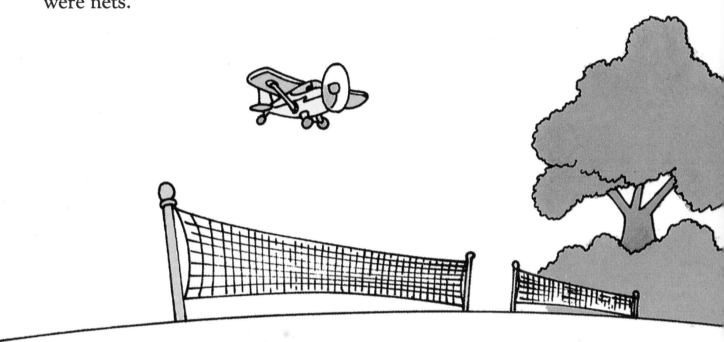

Mickey flew by the swimming pool, but all he saw was water.

He flew here and there, but he couldn't find his friends *anywhere*.

"Where can everyone be?" Mickey wondered. Suddenly, below him, he saw a big banner. The banner said,

WE MISS MICKEY!

And under the banner sat Minnie and Donald and Goofy and Daisy and Pluto. They were setting up their picnic.

Mickey grinned and waved. Then he landed his plane next to the banner.

"What a terrific message!" he told his friends. "I've missed all of you, too. I guess I got a little carried away with my flying lessons. But I'm glad I learned how to fly. It's fun!"

"Food's on!" called Daisy. They all sat down on a blanket and shared a delicious lunch.

"Now I have a surprise," said Mickey when he had finished eating. "I'm taking each of you for a ride in my plane."

"Oh, how wonderful!" said Minnie. And everyone cheered.

MICKEY MOUSE and GOOFY

The Big Bear Scare

"It's a beautiful day to go camping!" Mickey Mouse exclaimed as he locked the front door of his house.

"We're all ready to go, Uncle Mickey!" cried Morty. "Ferdie and I packed all the pots and pans and stuff we could possibly need."

"And *I've* packed enough food in my backpack for three days, Mickey!" Goofy said. "At first I couldn't get it all in, but I finally found room for everything."

Mickey smiled. "That's great! I'm glad we've all planned so carefully for this trip. The tent's ready to put up as soon as we get to our campsite."

"Uncle Mickey, let's follow the new bike trail out to the lake," Ferdie suggested.

"Okay, Ferdie," Mickey agreed. "That's a good idea."

The hike began well. Sunshine warmed the breeze,
and the birds sang happy songs. After a while, the
friends stopped to snack on some blackberries that
Goofy spotted growing beside the trail.

"I think this will be the best camp-out we've ever had," Mickey told his friends.

As Goofy turned around to agree he tripped over a log and sprawled on the ground. His bulging backpack came open, and everything in it tumbled out onto the grass.

"Oh, no!" Goofy groaned. "You fellows go on and find a good campsite. I'll repack this stuff and catch up as soon as I can."

"Okay, Goofy. We'll have everything set up for supper when you get there with the food," Mickey said.

"See you later!" the nephews called back from the trail.

While Goofy scrambled to put his pack together again, someone just out of sight watched with quiet interest. A hungry mother bear had come to visit her favorite berry patch. She stood behind a bush, only a few feet away from Goofy. Then, when his back was turned, she snatched the largest package and disappeared into the brush.

A few minutes later Goofy hurried to catch up with his friends, scratching his head in bewilderment. "This time everything fits into my backpack just right," he mumbled. "I wonder why."

"Hi, Goofy!" Mickey greeted his friend at the campsite. "Why don't you start supper while I finish setting up the tent? I'm almost done."

"We've already unpacked the pots and pans, Goofy.
We'll help you!" said Morty eagerly.

"Mountain air really makes you hungry, doesn't it,
boys?" said Goofy. "We'll have fish tomorrow, but
tonight we'll have the steaks I brought in my pack!"

Thinking how good the steaks would taste, Goofy hurriedly opened his backpack. "Here are the marshmallows, and here's the bread, the peanut butter, and the pancake mix. And here—" He stopped suddenly. "The steaks! The steaks are gone!"

"They can't be!" Mickey exclaimed.

"I must have left them at the place where my backpack fell open!" explained Goofy.

"Well," Mickey said, "that's not so bad. We'll just follow the trail back there and get them. Come on! Let's hurry!"

The four campers ran down the trail. When they came to the berry bushes, however, the missing steaks were nowhere to be found.

"I've spoiled the best camping trip ever," Goofy said sadly. "How could I have lost them?" He would not be comforted, no matter what Mickey and the nephews said to him.

Meanwhile, at the camp, three uninvited guests had arrived. The mother bear and her two cubs had come to visit. The cubs quickly discovered that banging pans together was fun. Their mother decided that the tent made a great den, and she settled down comfortably inside it.

"What's that racket?" Mickey wondered as they returned to their camp. Cautiously they hid in the brush nearby and peered into the clearing.

"Oh, no! Bear cubs!" Ferdie moaned.

"Shh!" warned Mickey. "Maybe they'll leave soon. It's funny they haven't eaten those marshmallows yet."

Suddenly Morty realized what must have happened to the steaks. "I'll bet they aren't hungry! *They're* the ones who ate our steaks!"

"Uncle Mickey!" Ferdie whispered. "Look! Something's moving inside our tent!"

"Grrrr," rumbled the mother bear softly as she turned over to lie on her other side.

"It must be the cubs' mother!" Mickey said worriedly. "How will we ever get her out of there?"

"I have to do something," Goofy thought.
"Otherwise, our whole trip will be spoiled—and
it will be my fault." He noticed a pail of water
near the firewood, and it gave him an idea.

While Mickey and the boys watched anxiously, Goofy crawled out of the brush, straight to the pail of water. He had never moved so quietly and carefully in his life. Grasping the pail, he slowly inched his way back into the brush.

"Now," Goofy thought as he hid behind a large tree trunk, "I'll climb this tree and dump the water on the bears. A shower should scare them away!"

However, the cubs had seen the pail disappear into the bushes and were watching for it to reappear. Soon they saw the pail moving slowly and jerkily up the side of a tree trunk!

"Here comes the mother bear!" Mickey warned. "She wants to see why the cubs are so quiet."

Climbing the tree was more difficult than Goofy had imagined. "I must be high enough now," he thought as he reached for an overhead branch. He peeked around the trunk and prepared to take aim. And what did he see? He saw all three bears—staring right at *him!*

Goofy was so frightened that he lost his hold on both the branch and the pail of water. "HELP!" he cried.

CRASH! SPLASH! Leaves, branches, pail and water, *and* Goofy all plunged down, flattening the tent!

Startled, the mother bear decided that she and her cubs had had enough of this strange place.

"The bears have left! The bears have left!" all four campers cheered with relief.

Goofy had saved the day.

MICKEY MOUSE
Those Were the Days

Mickey and his nephews were late arriving at Founders' Village, a landmark that showed what life was like in the olden days. There stood Mr. Bumbles, the caretaker, with his suitcase and his train ticket. He was all ready to leave on his vacation.

Morty and Ferdie ran to say good-bye to Mr. Bumbles. Mickey and the boys were to be the caretakers of Founders' Village while Mr. Bumbles was away.

"We know just what to do!" said Morty. "Every morning the horse gets hitched to the surrey. Then when all the people come, we'll take them for a surrey ride around the village."

"Afterward we'll serve homemade lemonade and popcorn," Ferdie said. "We'll make the popcorn on the wood-burning stove."

"Sounds like you have it down pat," said Mr.
Bumbles.

A taxi came up the hill, and Mr. Bumbles got in and
sped away.

"Won't this be fun!" cried Ferdie. "A whole week
living just the way our grandparents did."

"Those were the days, huh?" Morty chuckled as
they started for the stable to hitch up the horse.

The horse had other ideas. It would not go near the surrey, and it would not stand still. The horse pranced and stamped and reared. The boys scampered and prodded and pleaded, but they could not get the harness on the animal.

Mickey tried to help the boys. The horse made a snorting, whinnying noise at him. Then it trotted into the stable and wouldn't come out again.

Morty sighed. "Maybe nobody will want a surrey ride today," he said. "Maybe if we give people lots of lemonade and popcorn, they won't even remember we have a surrey."

"We can hope," said Mickey, but he didn't sound too hopeful.

Mickey and the boys went to the kitchen to start on the lemonade. Instead of a faucet, they found a pump for water. Mickey pumped the handle up and down, up and down. The pump rattled and squealed and squeaked, but not a drop of water came out.

Morty searched the cupboards. "Where's the juicer?" he cried. "And where's the outlet to plug in the juicer? We can't squeeze lemons without a juicer."

"We can't serve lemonade without ice, either," said Ferdie. "There are no ice cubes in this refrigerator."

"It's not a refrigerator," said Mickey. "It's an icebox, and it's empty.

"I'll go to town later and buy some ice," said Mickey.

"Could you buy some wood, too?" asked Morty. "The woodbox is empty."

"There's a woodpile behind the stable," said Mickey. "You know what that means?"

"Does it mean we're supposed to chop big pieces of wood into little pieces?" asked Ferdie.

Mickey grinned. "You're living in the good old days now, and in those days boys chopped wood."

The boys sighed, but they chopped the wood. Then
Mickey made a fire in the old stove.
For about three minutes the fire burned brightly.

Then smoke began to billow out into the kitchen.
"Uncle Mickey, the stove's on fire!" yelled Morty.
Mickey opened the stove lid. "Water!" he shouted.
"Get water! I'll put it out!"
But there was no water. The pump didn't work.

Ferdie coughed and choked. He pulled the front
door open. "I'll call the fire department!" he yelled.

He ran around Founders' Village, looking for a telephone, but there was none to be found. In the good old days people didn't have telephones.

By the time Ferdie got back to the house, the fire had died down. Mickey had thrown baking soda on the fire to put it out.

"That does it," said Mickey. "You two air out the kitchen. I'm going to town."

Mickey drove away toward town. When he came back, he had ice for the icebox.

"I made a couple of calls in town," Mickey told the boys. "Help is on the way."

Before long there was a rattling, clanking, chugging, puffing sound on the road. It was Goofy speeding to the rescue in his old car.

Minnie Mouse was with Goofy. So were Horace Horsecollar and Clarabelle Cow.

Clarabelle had once lived in the country, so she knew about wood-burning stoves. She turned a handle on the stovepipe. "That opens the draft," she said. "Now the stovepipe is clear and the smoke can go up the chimney."

Sure enough, when Mickey started a new fire in the stove, not a puff of smoke came out into the kitchen. Clarabelle started popping corn.

Minnie had never lived in the country, but she knew that lemonade was invented before people knew about electricity. She opened a cupboard and took out a funny-looking gadget.

"My grandma had a hand juicer, and it worked just fine," Minnie said. "This one should work, too. Ferdie, cut some lemons."

Ferdie did, and Minnie squeezed them on the hand juicer.

Horace Horsecollar fiddled with the pump. "I don't think it's broken," he said. "It just needs to be primed with water. It's a lucky thing I brought some water, just in case."

Horace carried a pail in from the car. He poured water from the pail into the pump. Then he moved the pump handle up and down.

This time the pump did not make an empty, rattling, squeaking sound. This time the pump gushed water.

"Great!" cried Morty. "Now we'll be all set if somebody can figure out an easy way to chop some more wood."

"No problem," said Horace. He led Morty and Ferdie out to the woodpile.

A car was pulling into a parking spot near the stable.
A mother and father were in the front seat of the car,
and two kids were in the backseat.

"Start chopping," Horace told the boys. "And
smile! You love to chop wood! You're having a great
time!"

"You've got to be kidding!" said Morty. But he and
Ferdie began to chop the wood with huge grins on their
faces. They even laughed out loud now and then as they
worked.

The kids from the car wandered over to see what was happening. After they watched for a minute, one of them said, "Hey, Dad, can I chop some wood?"

"You can if you promise to be very careful," said the father. "I'll stand here and watch."

"Oh, maybe you'd better not," said Morty.

"It's really hard work," added Ferdie.

But the kids begged and pleaded. Soon Morty and Ferdie gave up their axes and let the visitors chop the wood.

"Pretty smart, aren't you?" said Morty to Horace. "Maybe you know how we can hitch the horse to the surrey."

But Goofy was tending to the horse. He led the horse out of the stable, and he whispered something in the horse's ear.

The horse gave a startled snort. Then it backed up to the surrey and stood still, and Goofy hitched it up.

Presto! The surrey was ready for a load of passengers.

"What did you say to the horse?" gasped Ferdie.

"I told him if he wanted to lose his job, I could fix it for him," said Goofy. "I said that my jalopy is as old as anything in Founders' Village, but it will start easier than a stubborn horse, and people love to ride in it."

The rest of the day was grand.

The rest of the week was even better, with surrey rides and fresh lemonade and hot popcorn for everyone.

"The olden days really were good, weren't they?" said Ferdie.

"You bet," said Mickey. "But with good friends, any day is good."